At the Rooftop

A weekend adventure in sexual pleasure

Another erotic story

By

J.

Title ID: 3689410
ISBN-13: 978-0615541143

Rooftop Resort Hotel is an actual lifestyle resort in Hollywood Florida. All references to the hotel are with the permission of the owners of Rooftop Resort Hotel. Employees and guests mentioned in *At The Rooftop* are fictional. For more information on Rooftop Resort Hotel contact www.Rooftopresort.com or call   1 (800) 647-5426.

This is dedicated to all the fun people who have ever had a wild weekend at Rooftop Resort Hotel. You don't need to be named, you always will remember.

Chapter 1

The drop of perspiration ran down the back of Charlotte's neck before plunging between her shoulder blades. She felt it but chose not to move. The heat of the sun would dry the moisture, and it was just too hot to turn over. The sun was penetrating deep into her flesh, and she knew she'd pay the price for her lazy moment, especially on her naked ass that was not used to this much exposure.

For that matter, this weekend had all the indications it would produce a limelight to areas in her life not accustomed to this much disclosure.

Not that she had regrets or felt victimized; she'd come here willingly with her eyes wide open. It was simply different when you're living in the reality instead of living in the fantasy.

Letting out a long sigh, she finally rolled into a sitting position, feeling the small pool of perspiration trickle down her spine until it secured a resting place in the crack of her ass. Sensing the gentle breeze from the ocean, she stretched her body, once again regarding her new surroundings.

Sitting six floors above the hot Florida pavement, the resort was an inviting and relaxing place to drop out of the reality of life. It was an older hotel refurbished to fit the new owner's design. While rather plain and unobtrusive from the exterior, the interior had the atmosphere of a party. Vivid nudes on the lobby walls capped off a sign on the entrance stating, "Nude swimming is encouraged." Rooftop Resort Hotel was pure fun.

Charlotte was now on the hotel's top

6

deck where new guests were seeking the afternoon sun by rapidly occupying an area filled with chaise lounges. While the bar in the corner provided both shade and refreshment, the huge pool was the main attraction on the Rooftop's top deck. Skinny-dipping on the roof of a building with the other guests in the hotel was definitely a different experience. It's one thing to smile and be friendly, but when everything about you is out in the open, well that's different. Charlotte perused her own body, realizing the places not generally exposed to the sun were showing a bit of redness.

"You okay, baby?" the voice next to her asked. Charlotte reached out, stroked the naked back of her friend and smiled. "I'm okay, but we're both getting a little red. I'm going in the water for a minute and then heading to the bar. I think you should consider doing the same, Joey."

Pulling her sunglasses down, Joey leaned on her elbows. "I think you're right. I need a bathroom run, and then I'll join you in the pool." Setting a baseball cap on her head, Joey rose from the lounge and stretched. "What time is it anyway?"

Charlotte looked at her watch, "Three forty-five. That's two hours out here; it's shade time."

Standing, Joey checked out the area around the pool, observing the local inhabitants. Running her hand over her breast and down her belly, she smiled at Charlotte. "Okay, Char, be right back."

Charlotte watched Joey leave, once again admiring the muscular back which reflected months of working out in the gym. Joey wasn't as tall as Charlotte's five-seven frame, but her personality made her seem larger than life. With dark hair and beautiful green eyes, Joey was sexy, beautiful and fun. Her taught body remained a vivid testimony to all the hard work they'd put forth getting into shape.

Meeting during those grueling workouts at the gym, they'd slowly developed a strong, trusting friendship. The sexual part of their relationship grew as a gradual evolution, which had no actual beginning; just a series of moments weaving a pattern that beautifully fit together.

Charlotte smiled as she finally walked to the edge of the pool. One thing about being with Joey, you never knew where things would lead. Thus, here they were, naked in Florida, not really knowing why but definitely believing life was good. With that thought, she dove into the pool feeling the heat of her flesh cry out in relief.

Standing in the water, she did a few stretches to get the blood flowing in her muscles. They'd promised each other to exercise while on vacation, but as of day two, they hadn't even tried. She felt someone's hands go around her, squeezing her breasts. Recognizing both the finger rings, and the breast pressing into her back, Charlotte leaned into Joey's arms.

"You feel good, Char," Joey said as she wrapped her arms around Charlotte and held her. "Warm and slippery; my kind of woman."

Resting in Joey's embrace, Charlotte lifted her feet off the bottom. "I could get used to living like this," she murmured, as Joey slowly drifted her around the pool.

They'd made a last minute decision to flee the northern winter and head to Florida. Joey found an advertisement on the Internet for the Rooftop Resort Hotel in Hollywood,

10

Florida, a place catering to lifestyle living, which included a nude pool on the roof and clothing-optional throughout the hotel.

The hotel had about fifty rooms providing a very private, yet casual, atmosphere. Obviously catering to people in the freedom of sexual lifestyle, Rooftop provided an open and tranquil atmosphere to be and do whatever you wanted. It was close to the beach, but the lack of clothing only could take place within the hotel itself.

"You feeling more relaxed?" Joey asked as she continued to move around the shallow end of the pool.

"I'm very relaxed being with you," Charlotte said quietly, as she enjoyed resting in Joey's arms. "It's just those moments when I suddenly realize I'm totally naked among strangers that seems to throw me.

I guess too many years of being told to cover my body still rings in my head."

Joey pulled Charlotte close, squeezing her breast. "Anyone that looks as good as you do, deserves to be naked."

Charlotte had never been to the clothing-optional environment, so Joey convinced her it was time to break into new territory. She smiled as she thought back to the Charlotte she was a few years ago, knowing she'd come a long way.

Married too young to the wrong person almost destroyed her emotionally. She finished law school and filed for divorce the same month. As much as she tried to convince herself her husband was the problem, Charlotte knew she was also at fault. She'd married because her rather religious family expected it.

She wanted to simply live together for a

while and then decide, but finally succumbed to the pressure of her parents. That decision plunged her into an abyss, which almost sucked the life out of her. By twenty-four she was a divorced woman, thirty pounds overweight, and afraid to ever try relationships again.

Taking a job with a law firm in Manhattan, she left behind her broken life in Philadelphia. After a year of settling in the new job and environment of Manhattan, she finally joined the gym, beginning the long trek back to a healthy body.

Getting close to thirty, she now prided herself on her tight stomach and firm ass. Joey convinced her to lighten her hair to pure blonde, a move she was now happy to have made. Joey voiced her opinion that Charlotte's blue eyes deserved blonde hair, and Charlotte said okay. Even though she was afraid the blonde hair might give her a look of a brainless individual, Joey told her if anyone felt that way Charlotte really didn't need to be his or her friend.

"If I keep fondling you like this," Joey whispered softly, "I may have to make love to you in the pool."

Charlotte pulled Joey's arms tighter around her breasts. "You know I'm a sucker for your smooth lines, so I would probably go along with it. Nevertheless, we may want to behave before we get thrown out."

Meeting Joey began a physical transformation and an emotional metamorphosis. She and Joey loved each other deeply and intimately, but both knew they also desired to share their lives with men. Joey had never been married. Her goal was to stay single until she hit thirty and then start to find a permanent relationship with a man. It was a plan that made sense to Joey, so Charlotte didn't question it.

Meanwhile, Joey had a large group of close friends and dated quite easily. While Charlotte was still very hesitant about long-term commitment, she'd grown comfortable with dating around until she might discovered someone who might change her mind. Being with Joey was a safe place to explore her vastly improved outlook on life. Having just celebrated their twenty-eighth birthdays, neither of them was rushing into anything.

"I need a drink," Joey proclaimed as she released Charlotte and swam to the poolside. "I'll get a couple towels and meet you at the bar. Get me a Corona Lite."

Charlotte pushed up on the pool ledge, heading toward the bar in the corner. Noticing the arrival of a few more people, she began to feel a little self-conscious walking to the bar totally naked. Most of the other people were either undressed or heading in that direction. Nevertheless, it was still a rather new experience for Charlotte, and one that would take a little more practice. They arrived late Thursday afternoon, discovering most people came Friday through Monday in order to enjoy the long weekend in the sun. The good part about this was Charlotte's ability to ease into the surroundings without a lot of people around her.

Manny, the bartender, was busily loading up ice and glasses when Charlotte arrived.

"Hey, Charlotte, you through cooking in the sun?"

"Yeah Manny, I think I'm burning my butt and need to get into the shade. Can you fix two Corona with lime, and a bottle of water?

He smiled and set a bottle of water on

the bar. "You guys find something to do last night?"

Charlotte opened the water. "We went across the street for dinner, then just sat around the pool watching the stars."

Actually, she and Joey had partaken of a few too many margaritas at the bar and ended up having a great sexual romp on one of the canopy beds near the pool. She was sure there were others somewhere near them, but the passion and rum worked together to provide a façade of privacy.

Setting the two beers on the bar, Manny said, "Well, tonight will provide more people because Friday and Saturday are party times, so get your rest while you can. Got a great DJ Saturday night so should be a good weekend."

Joey walked up and threw the towels on the bar stools. "Whew, it feels a lot better in the shade! Look, I got sunburned on my tits, and I covered them with lotion!"

"See, that's what you get for making them so big." Charlotte laughed. Joey had implants about six months ago resulting in breasts that were about two sizes larger. While they were beautiful to look at, Charlotte decided she didn't like the feel as much and opted out of having it done. She was a nice 34c and happy with that.

"What's going on tonight, Manny?" Joey asked as she sat on the stool and took a large gulp from her beer.

"Reservations show about thirty new people coming tonight, so should be a good party. We're going to order pizza for everyone around six; that will give everybody a chance to meet and greet. You guys looking for others or are you just here as a couple?"

"Manny, "Joey said with a grin, "we are

into each other and whatever trouble we can find. This is a vacation, it is eighty degrees and we're naked. Honey, life is good."

Looking out over the rooftop of the hotel, watching the waves roll in on the beach, Charlotte smiled. *Life is good,* she thought, *very good.*

Chapter 2

Opening the door, Charlotte felt the refreshing cool air pour out of the room. Joey gave her a slight shove from behind. "Hurry up, I'm dying out here."

They entered their room, closed the door, and both lunged for the bed. "Oh my god," Charlotte said with a slight slur, "I'm smashed and it's only five o'clock. I only had two beers. How the hell did that happen?"

"It's the sun, baby," Joey said as she slipped off the bed and headed to the bathroom. "It dehydrates you, and beer's not a good hydrator."

Charlotte heard the shower start as she slowly sat up on the edge of the bed. The hotel recently refurbished the rooms into a modern Florida décor complete with vivid tropical colors. The rooms, all facing into the courtyard of the hotel, provided an abundance of sunlight and fresh air.

However, given the amount of heat today, the air-conditioned cool was a welcome and sobering relief. Listening to the water running in the bathroom, Charlotte decided a shower was a top priority.

Entering the bathroom, she stood for a moment enjoying the sight of Joey lathering her body under the streaming water. The Florida sun deepened Joey's New York spa tan into a vibrant brown, accenting the whiteness of her breasts and beautiful ass.

She watched as the water cascaded off Joey's slightly pink nipples, flowed down her brown, flat stomach, and finally formed a small river running through her smooth, shaved pussy. Joey was a beautiful woman who could be amazingly crazy or profoundly compassionate, depending on the situation.

Their first explorations into a sexual relationship came from Joey's caring conversations, as Charlotte walked through her shattered life. The beauty and gentleness of being together created a shared respect coupled with a desire to provide mutual comfort and happiness. In quiet moments, Charlotte still wondered how she'd become so much a part of another woman's life. Nevertheless, she always concluded that whatever the reasons, it was a good decision.

Looking at her beautiful friend glistening in the shower, Charlotte decided she needed to join her. Stepping into the glass-enclosed area with double showerheads, she gently touched Joey's back.

"Your butt's a little red, Joey. Am I burned?"

"You're a little red but not bad," Joey

said as she rubbed her hand over Charlotte's body. "In fact," she said as she drew Charlotte close, "you're not bad at all."

Charlotte pulled Joey's hair away from her face and lightly kissed her. "Florida sun makes you even more beautiful, Joe. We need to spend more time here."

Clinging to each other as the water rushed over their bodies, they kissed deeply, allowing their wet breasts to press together, providing a sensation that increased the intensity of their passion.

Lowering her head to Charlotte's breasts, Joey darted her tongue over her nipples until they were erect and sensitive. She then slowly pulled them into her mouth, sucking deeply.

Charlotte felt the hunger rush through her body, and then down her belly to her clitoris. The connection between her nipple and clit often amazed her. Discovering this connection over the last few years provided several new ways to experience sexual release, all of which she and Joey enjoyed exploring together.

Joey continued to stimulate her nipples as Charlotte placed a hand between her own legs, sensing the early pangs of a beginning orgasm. The feeling intensified as Joey persisted in extracting sensations from her breasts.

The water running down her body coupled with Joey's exploration drove Charlotte into frenzy. Thrusting her fingers inside, she felt the heat deep within herself. Her muscles tightened as she stimulated every pleasure point she could locate. Sensing the moment was now; she peaked and at last exploded. The waves of ecstasy flowed through her body as she thrust her fingers deeper into her vagina. Ultimately, the waves subsided as she leaned back against the wall.

"Feeling better?" Joey asked, lingering on Charlotte's nipples.

"Oh, that was a good start back to sobriety," Charlotte said softly, running her hands down Joey's back. "Now we need to help you go down the same road."

Placing her hands on Joey's shoulders, Charlotte gently turned her to face toward the wall. With the soap bar in her hand she began to rub Joey's back covering it with suds. The bubbles and slick film enclosed Joey in a rich cream, allowing Charlotte the ability to explore each muscle in Joey's taught back.

Reaching around, she took the soap, rubbed it over Joey's breasts and down her stomach. Extending her hands to the wall, Joey spread her legs slightly, providing room for Charlotte to slither soap across her muscled ass and between her cheeks. Turning the soap bar on edge, she slipped it between Joey's lips, running it gently on her clit until she felt it was hard.

Joey forced her body against Charlotte, spreading her legs to allow greater exposure. Charlotte dropped the soap, parted Joey's lips and entered her with her fingers.

Holding her close, Charlotte pushed up into Joey's warmth. Joey trembled and groaned as Charlotte probed deeper. She lightly touched her erect clitoris with her extended finger rapidly increasing Joey's excitement. "Oh, baby, do it to me!" Joey exclaimed as Charlotte moved her hand deeper and faster.

Reaching around with her other hand, Charlotte grasped Joey's breast firmly while she pushed her fingers in and out of Joey's wetness. Charlotte held Joey tight, pressing her own body into her as she massaged Joey's breast with her free hand.

"Oh, baby, yes, yes," Joey moaned, as her vaginal wall began to tense around Charlotte's fingers. Pressing back on Charlotte, Joey gasped as her body tensed.

"Oh fuck yes!" she screamed as the power of pleasure brought an ecstatic release. Pushing into Charlotte, Joey threw her head back, shivered and then lowering her arms, leaned back into Charlotte's embrace.

"Honey," Joey quietly whispered as they molded their bodies together in the waters, "You're the greatest."

"You taught me everything I know," Charlotte said softly. Joey turned and held Charlotte close. They continued to linger in each other's arms until Charlotte stepped back. Looking into Joey's vivid green eyes, she kissed her lightly, "Lets catch a nap and then head back up to the roof. Manny said they were ordering pizza, and I'm getting hungry."

"Sounds great," Joey said as she exited the shower, "but I want a snuggle nap, and I want to hold you."

Laughing, Charlotte said, "Your wish is my command, my love."

Chapter 3

The Florida sky was blazing with the colors of the sunset as Charlotte sat by the Rooftop Hotel cabana soaking in the last light of day. Although the evening was still warm, her sun-saturated skin felt the breeze as a slight chill, indicating clothing optional now meant that she opted for a light shirt. While it only came halfway down her butt, it was still some protection against the cool breeze.

"A beautiful woman, watching a beautiful sunset. A great combination."

Turning toward the voice, Charlotte discovered she didn't know the man who was speaking. He smiled and extended his hand. "I'm Charlie Kindle, but everyone calls me CK."

Charlotte grasped his hand and exchanged greetings. CK must have arrived while they napped, as he didn't look familiar, and she was sure she would remember if she'd previously seen him. He had a boyish look with soft features and light blond hair that highlighted his sun-darkened complexion, making his blue eyes appear electric. She guessed he was in his late twenties or early thirties.

"Mind if I join you?" he said, pointing to the chaise lounge next to her. "The view from here is fantastic."

She motioned him to take the seat but lost her thoughts as he took the towel from his waist and spread it on the lounge chair.

This sitting around naked was still a little strange to Charlotte; to suddenly be next to a completely naked male was a bit jarring. However, she did admire his build and couldn't help but notice that his male property was quite nice.

Leaning back, CK looked out at the breathtaking sunset. "We just got in and I needed to catch the sunset. I could see the low cumulous clouds and knew we were going to have a real color show."

She smiled and looked back at the sky. "I grabbed a nap and just got up here as the show started. It is spectacular."

"You here alone?" CK asked.

"No, my girlfriend, Joey, and I came down from New York yesterday. You with friends?"

"Yeah, I'm here with the two guys over by the pool," he said, motioning to two attractive men who were engaged in conversation with a woman in the pool. Glancing again, she saw the woman was Joey.

"They're talking to my friend Joey."

31

"I have to tell the truth. We met her in the pool and I asked if she knew who you were, so I already knew something about you. I'm never good at the first introduction thing, so I guess I didn't give you a true report."

She smiled. "You're forgiven. Just don't do it again. I forgive you 'cause I don't do well with first introductions either. Joey has no problem, so I usually just follow her."

Watching the setting sun for about a half hour, they exchanged small bits of information. CK owned some kind of Internet Company that did something with data, but Charlotte couldn't follow all he described. He lived in Tampa and indicated he'd been to the Rooftop Hotel a few times. CK was an easy conversationalist, and Charlotte relaxed with him as they enjoyed the splendor of nature being acted out before their eyes.

As the sky began to lose its color CK suggested they go to the bar, get a drink, and then join their friends in the pool. Charlotte checked on Joey, saw she had a fresh beer, and was obviously enjoying her conversation with CK's friends. Pulling up from the lounge chairs, they headed toward the bar, as CK once again wrapped the towel around his waist.

A few new people were drawn in by the pizza party, causing the bar area to become more crowded than earlier in the day. Charlotte noticed a lot of the guests were couples and the age of the crowd defied any set pattern. The night air brought out some clothing, but most were still in various stages of simply being happy, free, and naked.

"Hey, Charlotte, I see CK found you

quickly," Manny said with a smile, as they edged up to the bar. "I didn't think it would take long before you found some good people to hang out with."

"Does that mean CK is a good person, Manny, or did he pay you to say that?"

Manny laughed as he set their order on the bar. "CK is good. We get some strange people sometimes. A place like this is going to attract a few, but CK is always top drawer."

"Manny," CK said with a slight bow, "I'm indebted to you for your compliment."

"All tips are greatly appreciated," Manny said as he moved down the bar to take another order.

Leaning against the counter, Charlotte looked over the crowd gathered around the pool area. "This is truly a unique place. How often have you been here?"

"About six or eight times in the last couple years," CK replied. "We were here a few weeks ago, so I guess that's why Manny remembers me. Is this your first time here?"

"First time. Joey found the ad on the Internet and talked me into coming." She said, "Joey went to a place like this in Jamaica but this is my first time with the clothing-optional routine."

"You okay with it?" he asked.

"Surprisingly, I am. Joey and I went to a nude beach up in New York last summer, and I really enjoyed just being natural. There was no sexual connotation to the nude beach, and I have a feeling that isn't the case here."

CK smiled, "No, that's not the case here. Nevertheless, the bottom line is, no still means no, so you don't have to do anything you're not comfortable with and don't have to be with anyone who bothers you. It is just fun and freedom. Have you been in the lifestyle at all or is this all new to you?"

"Joey and I went to a club in Atlantic City, and she also has a couple of friends we party with once in a while, so I'm comfortable with some aspects of sexual freedom. I lived a more conservative life until I moved to New York and met Joey.

I sometimes wonder who I've become in the last few years, but all in all I'm happy with the new me. We've evolved into a more open sexual exploration even though I'm still cautious. In Atlantic City, we hooked up with a couple of girls and had a great time, so I'm becoming more open all the time."

"So you and Joey are a couple?" he asked, turning to look at her.

"We're best friends with great benefits,

but to answer the question you haven't asked, we're both bisexual, so guys also fit into our plans."

CK smiled and gave her a light hug. "Whew, I just had a moment of panic. I thought I had just found the perfect woman, but she wasn't into men."

Charlotte looked into his eyes and smiled. She found herself very comfortable with this man. He had an easygoing manner yet possessed an irresistible confidence. She was probably going to be sexually involved with him this weekend, a thought that brought both amazement and comfort at the same time. In the last two years, she'd become more casual with her sexual desires. Nevertheless, she remained somewhat cautious in the early stages of relationships. Aware of the obvious problems involved in casual sex, she set a firm ground rule that protected sex was the only sex she would have. Yet, here she was standing semi-naked with a semi-naked male, and she was positive she would become more than semi with this man.

Charlotte, she thought to herself, *what has become of you?* Deciding she really liked the new Charlotte, she reached up and lightly kissed CK. "Let's go see what trouble Joey and your friends are into at this point."

Walking over to the pool, they found Joey and several other people all standing and talking in the shallow end. Joey spotted Charlotte and waved to her. "Hey honey, come on in; the water is great."

Charlotte slipped out of her shoes, took off her shirt and stepped into the water, finding it delightfully warm. Joey reached out and pulling her close, gave her a big hug. "Where have you been? I looked over and you'd disappeared."

"It's my fault, Joey," CK said as he entered the water, "I kidnapped her and took her to the bar."

Joey looked at Charlotte and then back at CK. "I turn my back for one minute and look at the trouble you get into." She laughed and gave CK a hug. "Good move surfer boy, I told you she was fun." Turning to the people around her, she said, "Hey everyone, this is my best friend Charlotte. Introduce yourselves 'cause I don't remember half of your names yet, but I will in time."

Charlotte moved through the crowd of naked swimmers exchanging hugs and handshakes with the gathered group. Much like Joey, she only retained a few names. The majority of the people were married couples, but there were also a few single guys other than CK. He introduced her to his friends Rob and Mark, who had become very attached to Joey in a short time.

CK poured Charlotte's beer into a plastic cup and handed it to her. "So, welcome to the Rooftop Resort Hotel and the best pool in town."

Charlotte raised her glass and said, "Thank you, kind sir. It appears you have a very nice location here, and I must say everyone's bathing attire is quite nice."

CK put his arm around her and pulled her close. "I must say your bathing attire is one of the most attractive I've seen, and it does have a nice comfortable feel to it."

Charlotte felt the contact of his body, sensing an excitement move through her. Here she was, stark naked in the water, nothing but flesh all around her, with an attractive, sexy man holding her close. She really liked this Florida trip.

She slipped her arm around him and gave

a hug. Turning to face her, their lips met, and she tasted the warmth of his kiss. Holding her close, she felt her breasts press hard against his chest, causing a wave of erotic pleasure to curse through her body. Aware that he was also somewhat hard, she slid her hand from behind his back, gently grasping his erection. He was getting stiffer, and she could feel the throbbing as she held him. Finally letting go, she pulled back to look at him, "Well, it seems it is fairly easy getting to know a person in this pool."

He smiled. "That's why they don't have to heat the pool. We all just stand here and get hot."

"Hmmm,'" she said as she kissed him once more, "so far the water does seem a lot warmer."

Chapter 4

The party in the pool took on a life of its own. The more the drinks flowed, the more the pool became the place to be for a good time. Charlotte moved from group to group discovering the people were really a fun-loving, easy-going mix that simply enjoyed laughing, talking and being naked.

She spent time with CK's friends, Rob and Mark, determining they were all partners in the Internet Company CK previously tried to describe to her.

Rob was the oldest at thirty-eight, more serious and quiet than the other two partners, but still a fun personality. Mark was thirty-three, recently divorced and obviously quite intelligent.

In their conversations, Mark always

found some area of little-known facts that made the discussions quite lively. Joey was noticeably very fond of both men, leaving Charlotte to wonder how that would play out over the weekend.

Charlotte and CK circulated independently until they found each other at different parts of the pool. The more they drank, the more their greetings were like lost lovers who hadn't seen each other for years.

Running to each other, they'd embrace, kiss deeply, express long, enduring phrases to each other and then laugh hysterically. They were two independent spirits enjoying being free and able to find each other.

Charlotte believed she'd never laughed so much in her entire life. Not only were these people uninhibited, they all just enjoyed life and each other. Maybe it was the lack of pretense being naked provided, but something was definitely unique about these people.

The most intriguing part for Charlotte was the lack of overt sexual advances. The men and women were playful and periodically a couple would drift away to be more intimate, nevertheless most of the time it was just an open, fun, easy-going attitude.

Around midnight, couples began to drift off to their rooms leaving a slowly diminishing group. CK wandered over to Charlotte, who was sitting on the pool ledge talking to Joey and her "boys," Mark and Rob.

"I don't know about you guys," he said as he sat next to Charlotte, "but if I stay in this pool much longer I'll turn into a prune. Let's go someplace warm and dry."

"We have beer, booze, and food in our room," Rob chimed in, "and I understand it is warm and dry."

Joey looked up at Charlotte. "What are you up for, honey? Want to go with them or are you finished for the day?"

Charlotte hesitated for a minute, aware that going back to the room with the guys would probably entail more than beer and food. The difficulty was, she didn't really know what to expect but on the other hand, she really didn't feel like she was in unsafe territory. "If you're up for it, Joey, I am too."

Exiting the pool, they began a search for various articles of shoes, clothing and towels before heading down to the rooms. CK, Rob and Mark occupied adjoining units on the floor below the pool deck. As promised, they had enough beer, booze and snacks to feed an army. On the way to the room, they observed a few couples collected in different stages of intimacy, seemingly unconcerned that the curtains were open allowing for some interesting views. Passing a room with some very hot activity taking place inside, Charlotte commented this was a voyeur's paradise.

Mark indicated the second floor now housed a new club with a band, playrooms, and full bar that would be open on Saturday night. This piece of information caused Joey to let out a yell and proclaim, "Let the party continue!"

In the room, Rob had an iPod player with some good, mellow music. Surprisingly, he was an Eric Clapton fan with a large cross-section of Clapton and Cream songs. Listening to the music, Charlotte closed her eyes as she slowly moved to the rhythm. CK put his arm around her and asked if he could join the dance.

The feeling of flesh on flesh was exhilarating as they held each other tightly, slow dancing to Clapton singing, "Bell Bottom Blues." Feeling his erection pressing against her belly, she sensed an arousal of her own, causing her to feel moisture between her legs.

"This is a very interesting way to dance," Charlotte whispered as their bodies continued to press together.

"Are you okay?" CK asked pulling back to look into her eyes.

Smiling, she kissed him and then replied, "I'm feeling better every second."

Grasping her breast in his hand, CK provided a gentle massage triggering her nipple to become hard and sensitive. As he held her breast, Charlotte moved her hands around to her belly, grasping his hot steel-hard erection. Glancing over her shoulder, she observed Joey and her "boys" had now taken a horizontal position on the bed and were deeply lost in their own journey.

Massaging his throbbing dick, she slowly began to move down his body until her knees touched the soft carpet. His rigid penis was now before her, allowing her to kiss it lightly as she worked her lips up and down the shaft.

Opening her lips, she took him into her mouth, running her tongue around his hot dick. Pulling him deeper into her mouth, she slowly drew back until he was out. Taking a step back, CK sat on the edge of the bed. She followed, once again pulling him deep into her mouth as she ran her hands over his body enjoying the tightness of his muscles and the strength she felt in him.

Releasing him from her mouth, she ran his hard cock down her neck and between her breasts where she held it tightly as she moved to the rhythm of the music. Reaching down, he took her head in his hands, pulling her up toward him, and then kissed her deeply.

"I need to explore you," he said softly. "I want to touch and taste every part of your body."

Lifting Charlotte in his arms, he laid her on her back enabling her to watch him as he slowly moved down her figure, slowly touching her with his fingers and tongue, causing her breath to become quick and shallow.

Looking over to the other bed, Charlotte watched Joey passionately enjoy a three-way oral orgy. Rob was between her legs bringing Joey gratification as she was slowly giving oral pleasure to Mark's rather large erection.

Charlotte felt CK's tongue touch her clit and a vibration went through her until it hit her nipples. As he continued to run his tongue around her clit, she squeezed both her nipples, giving way to what she knew would be the first of many big "O's" that night. Running his tongue around her smoothly shaved pussy, he spread her lips and slipped his fingers inside.

The passion grew as she turned to watch Joey, who was just on the edge of orgasm. Feeling CK's tongue and fingers probe her from every direction, she watched her friend arch her back as Rob fingered her pussy while he sucked on her clit. Immersed in watching her best friend's passion grow, Charlotte felt her own craving increase until her entire body seemed filled with fire and ice.

She held on tight, waiting, waiting, and then as Joey exploded, she allowed her own climax to surface. CK pushed two fingers deep inside her, while he squeezed her clit in his lips. Charlotte erupted, feeling the wetness of her own cum flood out of her, covering her pussy and ass. Continuing to press on her clit with his hand, CK drew Charlotte out until she sensed her body detonate several more times. Grasping her breast, she pressed her pussy into his hand, tensed, then felt the explosive pleasure deep in her vagina. Finally, positive that if she had one more orgasm she would die, Charlotte collapsed on her back, totally spent. CK moved up the bed and pulled her close. Wrapping her leg over him, she relaxed in the comfort of his embrace, slowly drifting into a post-climax sleep.

Awakening later, she had difficulty acclimating herself. Glancing to the other bed, she spotted Joey lying next to Rob but couldn't see Mark anywhere. CK, lying next to her, breathed deeply, obviously sound asleep. Quietly, she slipped out of bed and knelt next to Joey. Shaking her lightly, Joey's eyes opened. Smiling she said, "Hey, Char, having a good vacation?"

"Great vacation, but why don't we head back to our room for the rest of the night? I think the party's over here."

"Okay, honey," Joey said quietly as she slipped off the bed. "Lead and I will follow."

Charlotte laughed to herself as they exited the room, heading down the stairs to their own place. Joey may do a lot of things in life, but follow was not one she often pursued.

Chapter 5

Charlotte was sure she was sweating out beer as she ran down the beach. This was a great vacation, but it didn't fit in well with her physical discipline.

When she woke about eight this morning, she knew it was not an option to skip a couple-mile run. Joey opted to do laps in the pool but seemed to be in bed thinking about it when Charlotte left the room.

She knew she was getting into the routine of being naked when it was a real bother to get dressed for the morning run.

Exiting the building, she felt like everybody was looking at her, knowing she was one of those sex people who stayed at Rooftop Resort. In all honesty, there wasn't anybody around when she left the hotel, so the accusing voices were only in her head. She stretched for a minute and then headed down the street toward the boardwalk.

The area around the hotel was a throwback to the 70's. Small hotel units filled the adjacent streets, advertising efficiency suites available for the week or the month. The boardwalk appeared to be more upscale and expansive.

Charlotte crossed the walkway and headed down to the solid sand along the oceanfront beach.

There were a few stragglers around who were just beginning a new day at the beach but for the most part the area was spacious with beautiful white sand and the most picturesque clear-blue water she'd ever seen.

Jogging down the beach, she saw the high-rise hotels and condos further away, but for the most part, Hollywood beach was simply a quiet part of paradise.

Last night had been a lot of fun, both
in the pool and in CK's room. The concept of
a clothing-optional resort being one large
orgy was really false. Oh sure, sex was part
of the surroundings, but sex was usually part
of any hotel. It was just more out in the
open here. The people she met were just fun.
She hadn't laughed so hard in a long time,
and never felt like she was being hassled for
sex. All in all, it was a good experience.

She finished her five-mile run, headed
back to the hotel, making a direct route to
the pool. The pool area was mostly empty,
however, she found Joey doing laps as she had
promised.

Charlotte stripped off her sweaty top
and shorts, dove into the water, and waited
for Joey to come to the shallow end. As Joey
approached, Charlotte stepped into her lane.

Joey hesitated slightly, and then dove under water, giving Charlotte a big kiss between her legs. She surfaced laughing and splashing on Charlotte. "I'd know that pussy anyplace, even underwater," she laughed, "How was your run?"

"It was great, but I think I drank too much last night. May have to go easier today."

"Sure, sure. That's what every drunk says the morning after. Come on, Char, let's go get something to eat. I'm starving."

They ran back to the room, threw on some clothes and then headed out to the boardwalk for breakfast. The sun was already warming, providing the promise of another perfect vacation day. There were several breakfast places right on the boardwalk, so they chose an outdoor table providing a great view of the boardwalk and the ocean.

Charlotte noted that the age of the population was definitely closer to retirement years. The fascinating part was, no matter what the age, everybody looked healthy and very much alive. In New York City, the population seemed to move about in a zombie-like state, precluding much interaction or feeling of life. She thought she might want to consider moving out of New York and heading south but decided to hold that thought for another day.

After they ordered, Charlotte sat back and asked, "So, how did you like last night?"

"Honey, it was a great time. I love the people in the pool. Rob and Mark took me into a great place, and I really had a big "O"."

"I know. I watched you while CK was turning me on with some great oral moves. I held out on my climax until I saw you explode. You looked fantastic and turned me on as I watched you. That's the first time I ever saw you with a man, and it was hot. Did you have intercourse or just what I saw?"

"I didn't go all the way, I fell asleep after I exploded. I do know Mark climaxed. I was sucking on him when he did. Don't think Rob did, at least not with me. What about you?"

Charlotte smiled, "I fell asleep too and I think I may have a very horny CK on my hands today. We did a lot of messing around, but I'm the only one who got release. Hope I didn't piss him off."

"Hey, it's a long weekend. If he gets upset with that, then we'll find someone else. I really wish I'd watched you. I was a little buried in my work." Joey laughed. "I really want to watch you, Char, so let's keep that in mind. Damn, girl, we've got to change the subject or I may have to make love to you right here."

Their order came and between the food and other distractions, they survived without succumbing to sex on the breakfast table. Finishing their meal, they did a little shopping on the boardwalk, and then headed back to the hotel. In the lobby, which was busy with new people arriving, Joey noticed a sign stating, "See Lee about massage schedule for today."

"I think we owe it to ourselves to get a massage," Joey said. "Let's see if Manny can point us to Lee so we can get scheduled."

"Sounds good," Charlotte said, "but let's get rid of these packages and clothes. See--I'm becoming a real nudist; can't wait to get naked."

"Be sure you cover that beautiful ass with sunscreen," Joey said. "If I'm going to watch you get laid, I don't want a red ass bouncing all over the bed."

The pool area was picking up clientele, and would definitely be crowded by the afternoon. Joey went to check with Manny about the massage man, as Charlotte found a couple chaise lounge chairs near the pool. There was a couple next to them that she remembered from the pool last night, and they greeted each other like close friends. She remembered the woman's name was Jackie but couldn't remember the husband's name. They were in their late forties and had been married for some time. Charlotte recalled they were from Cleveland, Ohio, but couldn't come up with much more.

Joey arrived, greeting everybody she saw, including Jackie and her husband who received big hugs. She called him Roger, so at least Charlotte had that part of the puzzle fixed.

Joey settled next to Charlotte and said, "We're scheduled for one o'clock this afternoon. He'll set it up so he can do both of us together. Nice guy. Told him we wanted to learn some massage techniques to use on each other and he said he would show us. I'm excited!"

Charlotte laughed and hugged her friend. Joey loved life, new adventures and sex, not necessarily in that order. "Sounds like fun. Where does all this take place?"

"He gave me two options," Joey said as she liberally applied sun lotion to her breasts. "We could either use the cabana over there or we could use our room. I thought about how hot it may be at one in the afternoon and decided our room would be best."

Charlotte was about to agree with Joey's plan when a shadow moved over her. Looking up she saw CK standing before her with his beautiful manhood well displayed. Remembering her encounter with his erection caused a momentary rush to go through her body.

"So, gorgeous woman," he said as he sat next to her lounge, "I woke up this morning and found myself all alone. I don't remember you leaving, and I'm very hopeful we didn't have any problem that caused you to flee into the night."

She sat up, put her arms around his neck and kissed him. "No, my wonderful man, you treated me very well. In fact, you treated me so well I fell asleep, and when I woke up you were asleep. Joey and I decided to retreat to our room but simply out of convenience not because of a problem."

He hugged her and let out a deep sigh, "What a relief. Rob couldn't remember you leaving and Mark apparently went up to the rooftop and fell asleep on the lounge until this morning. I called your room but got no answer."

"I went for a run and Joey worked out in the pool, so you probably missed us."

"Well, it is almost noon and I need a drink. Can I get you two anything?"

"I'll pass for now," Charlotte said.

"Thanks, me too," Joey replied. "We're doing a massage at one, and I'm going to hold off until that's over."

"You going to have Lee give you a massage?" CK asked as he stood.

"Yeah, is he any good?" Joey asked.

CK laughed, "I never had a massage with him, but let's say the women who have all seem to have a very nice smile when they're finished. I'm going to go grab a beer, and then we're going up to the boardwalk to get some lunch. Catch up with you after your massage?"

"That sounds like a perfect plan," said Charlotte. "I'll be relaxed and ready to party."

CK leaned over and kissed her. "Don't get too relaxed and fall asleep again. I still want to spend some quality time with you. Watch out for the happy endings with the massage, they can wear you out." He chuckled, kissed her again and then left.

"He is obviously not pissed," Joey said. "So you can rest your mind about that. Does happy ending with the massage mean what I think it means?"

Charlotte smiled, "I know how you think and I think you're probably right. Guess we will just have to see."

Joey closed her eyes and stretched out in the sun, "Oh, I am so excited."

Chapter 6

Charlotte was just getting out of the shower when she heard a knock on the door. Joey got up from the bed to answer it. Glancing at the clock, she saw it was one o'clock, so anticipated it would be Lee to give the massage. They'd sat in the sun until about fifteen minutes ago then decided to freshen up before Lee arrived.

Lee entered the room, and all Charlotte could see was a smile. He was one of the darkest people she'd ever met, with a smile that was as big and bright as the moon in a clear sky.

Joey pointed to Charlotte. "Lee, this is my friend Charlotte, who I told you about."

Lee set a large folding table on the floor and threw open his arms. "Come give Lee a hug, my beautiful woman. I do believe the gods have made my day. One competent but lonely man locked in a room with two beautiful women. Oh, it is a wonderful life."

Charlotte laughed and hugged Lee, as he enveloped her with his huge arms. With arms the size of most people's legs, and shoulders she regarded as mountains, Lee looked like he played professional football. Taking this rather large man into her total view, Charlotte was a little concerned about how rough this massage was going to be.

"So you two want to learn how to do some massage on each other. I like that. Good to teach. Good to do. Who goes first?"

"I will," Joey said, "I've been looking forward to this all morning."

Lee began to set up his table and put a long sheet over it. "Sweet Charlotte, put this CD in the player over there. It will help us be in touch."

Charlotte complied and soon a gentle, almost spiritual sound filled the room. Joey threw off her towel and lay down on the massage table. Lee took off his shirt allowing Charlotte to confirm that this man was built out of pure granite. Pouring oil onto his hands, he rubbed them together, and then began to spread it over Joey's back. Charlotte sat in a nearby chair watching as he slowly worked over Joey's shoulders, arms, hands, back and lower back. As he applied oil to Joey's butt cheeks, he motioned Charlotte to come over.

Cupping Joey's cheeks in his hands he squeezed and pressed down. Placing his thumbs on the bottom of her spine he said, "All the nerve endings come to this place. Between the end of her spine and the tip of her sphincter, there are thousands of nerves that bring pleasure."

He pressed on the area with his thumbs, and she heard Joey moan. Spreading her cheeks apart, he ran his finger down her thighs but very carefully avoided touching her vulva. He pushed in hard all around her lips but evaded contact.

Taking Charlotte's hands, he placed them on Joey's cheeks. "Now you try it. Press down and place your thumbs deep below the spine." Charlotte complied, and Joey once again let out a moan.

Placing his hands on hers, he began to descend Joey's inner thigh, once again avoiding touching her lips. He continued to hold Charlotte's hands as she ran them down Joey's thigh and calf.

"You did well, Charlotte. It is a good place to help relax. Now change spaces, and we will see how Joey does."

Reluctantly, Joey sat up and moved off the table. "Oh baby, my pussy is singing and needs a touch."

"It is good to feel that," Lee said as he began to spread oil over Charlotte's back. "The best part of being in touch with yourself is feeling your lower chakra and sensing its desire."

Charlotte felt the depth of Lee's touch as he worked on her arms and back. He had a gentle yet firm touch, but his hands were so soft they felt like silk. She wondered how someone so big and tough could have such gentle hands. She felt him put oil on her buttocks as he called Joey to the table.

As he massaged her cheeks, she tuned out of the conversation and simply got lost in the feeling. Sensing his fingers at the base of her spine, she felt him push in, and she realized a rush of pleasure extending from

70

his fingers right up her ass and into her stomach. She groaned at the sensation.

She then experienced Joey beginning to rub her, and she got lost in the ecstasy of both their hands rubbing her inner thigh. She desperately wanted them to touch her vagina and almost reached back to do it herself, but then their hands went down her legs and she relaxed.

"So, how do you two feel?" Lee asked as he helped Charlotte to her feet.

"I feel relaxed but also hotter than hell," Joey said, grabbing her pussy.

Lee took out another sheet and spread it over the king-size bed. He took Joey's hand and had her recline on her back, pulling up her left leg. Then he had Charlotte lie on the bed so her feet were at Joey's shoulders. Lifting Charlotte's left leg, he pulled the two women together so their vulva lips could touch.

"Press together until you feel the heat from your partner," he directed. The two women pressed in as they both began to feel the heat coming from each other. Joey ground her hips, pushing hard on Charlotte. They both were wet, and their lips moved smoothly across each other. Charlotte, feeling Joey press on her clit, was amazed at how hard and erect it had become.

Lee placed his hands gently on each of their legs and quietly said, "Now stay close and only move small amounts when you feel the need."

He took out a lighter and warmed a small spoon on which he placed a honey-colored liquid. He turned the spoon over so the liquid ran between their legs and over their pressed-together vulva lips. Charlotte felt the warmth, and then she began to feel like a thousand fingers were touching her clit. She sensed Joey press in on her and knew she was feeling the same thing.

"Put your hands on your breasts and massage them," he requested softly. He again took out the lighter and warmed a thick, black liquid. Placing the spoon over their combined pussies, he allowed the warm liquid to drip slowly.

The feeling that came over Charlotte was someplace between orgasm and drunk. She experienced the heat from Joey, and her clit throbbed. Charlotte squeezed her own breast so hard it hurt, but she continued to do it.

"Now slide your fingers into the space between your legs and feel each others fingers and warm lips."

Charlotte felt Joey touch her and almost exploded. Their fingers caressed as she felt the stiffness of Joey's clit.

Lee leaned over and whispered quietly, "Lay face to face now and bring your partner to completion."

Joey rolled toward Charlotte, grabbed her breast with one hand, and her pussy with the other. Fire raced through their bodies as they both plunged deep into each other, frantically penetrating and stroking the other's lips and clit. They rolled over each other, neither letting go, each begging for more. Suddenly, as if a switch was thrown, they knew they were going to cum. Pressing deep inside, each tensed, pushed, grabbed, and finally exploded in a scream of ecstasy. Holding each other, fingers buried deep in their partner's throbbing vagina, each experienced wave after wave of sexual release. Finally, unable to hold on, they rolled to their backs and lay panting.

"Holly Shit!" Joey moaned. "What in the

hell was that stuff?"

Lee laughed and softly said, "A gift from the islands."

"Tell the islands thanks," Charlotte moaned.

"They say you're welcome," Lee whispered as he kissed each of them gently, packed up his table, and left.

Chapter 7

Charlotte felt CK spread lotion on her back and over her ass. "Thanks, I think I fell asleep again," she said quietly.

"That must have been some massage." CK laughed as he continued to rub lotion on her body. "You and Joey have been like zombies ever since you came back to the roof. Must have been a very happy ending."

Charlotte shifted so she could look up at CK.

"It was great, but he didn't have sex with us; he just set us up so we really enjoyed each other." Leaning back, she recalled the wonderful time she had just experienced.

"He had some kind of lotion he said was from the islands. When he put it between our legs, we went crazy. I think I exploded from my toes to my teeth! Guess that's why we're so worn out at this point." She laughed, "Just getting up the stairs from our room was a miracle."

CK put the cap on the sun lotion, reached over, kissed her lightly and said, "I hope you're not totally worn out."

Charlotte kissed him back. "I will recover, I promise."

"I think if you got us both a drink, we'd be better," Joey murmured as she turned over onto her back. "It's almost three o'clock, and I'm ready to get into a party mood."

"Your wish is my command," CK said as he

jumped to his feet and saluted Joey. "I'm going to wake up Mark in the room, then I'll grab you whatever you want."

They both ordered a beer, and CK headed down the stairs to fulfill their request. Joey reached over and took Charlotte's hand. "Hey, baby, that was one hell of a ride we went through. I soaked myself when I came. I never got that wet before."

Charlotte whispered back, "I know, my fingers were deep in you when you let loose. I didn't pay attention as I was just a little distracted with my own orgasm, but when I finally came around, I realized you were soaking me. I know you sometimes squirt, but Joey, that was a geyser!"

They both laughed as Joey adjusted her lounge chair and sat up. "I have to talk to Lee and see if we can get some of that lotion. We could have a lot of fun with it in our toy box."

Turning around she stood and proclaimed, "I'm getting the shit fried out of me. Come on, let's get in the pool and cool off."

The two of them entered the pool and felt the cool water penetrate their hot flesh. Charlotte dove to the bottom and then pushed up to do a few laps. Between the morning run and the afternoon sex massage, she felt whole again and surprisingly was ready to join Joey in her quest for party time. She came into the shallow end as CK entered the pool carrying two cold cans of beer.

"My hero," Joey exclaimed as she took one and gave CK a big kiss.

"Nothing better than being greeted by a wet, naked, grateful woman," he said as he handed the other can to Charlotte.

Charlotte and Joey came close to CK,

reached under the water simultaneously, seizing his manhood into their grasp. "See how grateful two wet, naked women can be," Charlotte murmured, kissing him deeply. They both pulled close and continued to stroke his rapidly growing erection. Taking a deep breath, he quietly exclaimed, "And what are these two grateful women going to do now that they have me all turned on?"

Joey laughed as she released him and headed toward the stairs. "We are going to go oit and enjoy our beer as we watch you and your erection get out of the pool."

"Damn," he said as he slowly leaned against the pool edge and tried to relax. "You two are just trouble."

"Yeah," Charlotte smiled, "but we're really worth the trouble."

The afternoon sun gave way to the warm,

late afternoon tropical shower that almost daily drifts through southern Florida. Manny turned up the stereo and the assembled guests either ducked under the umbrellas or headed into the pool. Rain or shine, the party would continue. It took about a half hour for the showers to end as the beautiful afternoon sun provided a spectacular array of color, including a double rainbow over the ocean.

It was Saturday night Bar-B-Q and the smell of grilled hamburgers and hotdogs soon filled the air. Joey and Mark set up a table as Charlotte and CK filled plates for all of them. Rob hooked up with a couple from Rhode Island and it appeared they were going to spend some quality time together that night; one of the advantages of being with people who just loved living life to the fullest. While not all the married couples were at Rooftop Hotel for sex play with others, enough were so that night activities were made interesting.

CK and Charlotte brought the food to the table, only to discover Joey had invited a couple she'd befriended the day before. Charlotte remembered the woman named Pam, a beautiful, sexy, blond about thirty-eight, who was from St. Louis. Her husband, a slim and attractive man with a great sense of humor, was named Brad.

Charlotte brought over towels for the chairs, as she was still not inclined to put her bare bottom on a place where other bare bottoms had just been seated. She smiled, considering that she might have sex with a person but didn't want to sit on a chair they'd vacated. That just wasn't logical, but considering the weekend so far, nothing was really logical.

As they all sat enjoying the company and

food, Pat looked over to Charlotte and asked, "So I'm curious. Are you and Joey a couple or just friends?"

Charlotte smiled. "Joey's the closest friend I have in the world, and she is also someone I enjoy being with sexually. The friendship came first and the sex grew out of it."

"So you are both bisexual?" Pam asked.

"Yep," Joey chimed in, "we've got the best of both worlds. What about you Pam, you bi or just straight?"

Pam hesitated for a minute, and then Brad laughed. "The love of my life is bi-curious, with the emphasis on curious."

"So you've thought about it but have never done it," Joey said.

"When I was in college I had a one-night drunken stand with a female friend, but never repeated it," Pam said. "Last time we were down here I was going to try but backed down at the last minute."

"Why'd you back down?" Charlotte asked.

"I don't know. Well that's not true, I do know. I just didn't understand what to do and not wanting to feel stupid, I backed out."

"Honey," Joey said, taking Pam's hand, "you just have to do to your partner what you want to have done to yourself. You know what feels good to a woman more than these knuckle-dragging men do."

Almost with one voice, CK, Brad and Mark began to chide Joey about her remark. Brad finally laughed and said, "I may drag my knuckles but I also know a lot of things a woman likes."

"That's the truth," Pam said. "I love sex with my husband, and while we have shared with a few other couples, it's always the best feeling to be with Brad. However, I think that's why I'm curious. I think part of me also wants to be expressed in a different way, but I just don't let it loose."

"Want to go back to the room and find an answer to your question?" Joey asked.

"Wait," Brad asked, "just what are we supposed to do while you three go play? I mean, I like these two men, but not that much."

Joey smiled as she stood and took Pam's hand. "If you three can sit and watch without touching or interfering, then you're free to come too. Okay with you, Pam and Charlotte?"

They both said yes, and the party moved from the pool to the room.

Chapter 8

Joey brushed the hair from Pam's neck,
kissing her gently, while Pam reclined on the
bed between her and Charlotte. "The key to
making love is just to enjoy the moment,"
Joey said softly. "If you want something just
say it. If you don't, just say that too."

Pam hesitated, then reached over and
caressed Charlotte's breast. Charlotte moved
closer so Pam could embrace her breast and
nipple. "Suck on me," Charlotte said softly
and lifted her breast to Pam's mouth.

Running her tongue over Charlotte's
erect nipple, Pam placed her lips around the
firm mound, sucking hard, until she had about
half of Charlotte's breast in her mouth.
Slowly releasing it, she took both breasts in
her hands and pulled the nipples close

together.

She ran her tongue around both nipples and then sucked on them simultaneously. Charlotte felt a rush run through her body that took her breath away. As Pam continued to pull Charlotte's excited nipples into her mouth, Joey moved her lips down Pam's neck to her breast.

Massaging each one deeply, Joey could feel the softness of Pam's natural breasts and discerned that this size 36 was totally real. Grabbing the left one in both hands she squeezed until the nipple turned a dark red. Placing her mouth around Pam's hardened teat, she ran her tongue around it, and then pinched it gently with her teeth. Holding the erect nipple in her teeth, Joey released her grip sucking the hard nipple into her mouth. Pam let out a quick breath, releasing Charlotte's breast and falling back.

"Oh my god, this is what I've been waiting for." She reach up, kissed Charlotte, and then lay back as Joey ran her fingertips down Pam's belly, lightly touching between her legs. Pam was smooth shaved, as were Joey and Charlotte. Pam spread her legs, as Joey pressed down on her clit.

Opening Pam's legs further, Joey slowly slid her finger into the warmth of her vagina. Pam lay back and began to moan, unable to suck on Charlotte's breast. Charlotte slid down and began to massage Pam's breast as Joey pushed deeper, slipped in another finger, pressed her thumb on Pam's clit, and pushed hard. Pam arched her back letting out a loud gasp. Unable to stop, she held Charlotte tight as she gave way to her ecstasy.

Finally releasing Charlotte, Pam dropped her hands on the bed and relaxed. "Holy shit," she sighed, "that was fun and a half."

Joey kissed her and then rolled on top. "That was a good start, but I need to see how well you really know a woman's body." Looking up at Charlotte she smiled, rolled off of Pam, and reclined on her back, saying, "Why don't you to check my oil and make sure my engine is in working order." Charlotte laughed and motioned Pam to follow her down Joey's body.

"What Joey's asking for is to check under her hood," Charlotte said as she spread Joey's legs, placing them far apart, while she and Pam sat in between. Gently holding Pam's hand, she placed it just above Joey's clit. "Put your thumb on her clit and pull the skin up," she said softly. Pam complied, exposing Joey's erect clitoris.

"See," Charlotte said softly, "That's under the hood. Now I'll check her oil."

89

Saying this, she leaned close, touching Joey's exposed clit with her tongue. Running her tongue around it, she finally pressed it between her lips as Joey let out a gasp.

Charlotte lightly touched the clitoris, again causing Joey's pussy lips to slowly expand, displaying a beautiful wet opening Charlotte could now gently enter with her two fingers.

Joey gasped again as she spread her legs even further, pushing her pussy on Charlotte's fingers. Charlotte pulled out and then looked at Pam. "Everything seems good to me, see what you think."

Pulling Joey's hood even higher, Pam lowered her lips to the now hard and erect clit. Taking it between her lips, she opened her mouth wider, surrounding the entire area.

Running her tongue around Joey's clit, she moved faster and faster as Joey arched her back and began to tense. Continuing to work on Joey, Pam placed her fingers between Joey's lips and thrust in hard and deep. Joey let out a scream as she arched her back, pressing her pussy deep into Pam's mouth. With another gasp, Joey exploded and clamped her legs around Pam's head as she continued to have multiple orgasms. Pam continued to hold Joey's clit between her lips until Joey finally released Pam from between her legs and pulled her up.

"Are you sure you never did this before?" Joey asked as she tried to catch her breath.

"Hey, you told me to do things I like," Pam said, giving Joey a hug. "And that is something I really like."

"Well, welcome to the world of bi-sexual," Joey exclaimed, "You are no longer just curious."

"Charlotte's next," Pam said with excitement. "What do you want?"

Before Charlotte could answer, Joey sat up and said, "I know what she wants."

Charlotte just shrugged and laughed. "I'm a slave to this woman, I do what she wants."

Telling Charlotte to lie on her stomach, Joey reached into the drawer next to the bed. Charlotte looked up as Joey pulled out a dildo and a bead chain. "Oh oh, my ass is grass." She laughed and then put her head down on the pillow.

"What's that?" Pam asked, pointing to the bead chain. The chain was a flexible plastic with several balls attached to it. The one end was a small ball, then each one increased in size until the last one in the chain, which was about an inch in diameter.

"That will be used to send my beautiful

friend into a climax that will curl her toes," Joey said.

Joey told Charlotte to pull her legs up under her, allowing full access to both pussy and ass. Twisting the dildo, it began to vibrate. She handed it to Pam, saying, "You work the lower area. I'll do the upper."

Pam began to slowly run the vibrator around Charlotte's exposed pussy lips. Pressing lightly, she slid the vibrator in, as Charlotte let out a quiet moan. Joey took some lotion, letting it run over Charlotte's ass and down her pussy.

Rubbing the lotion on Charlotte's rectum, she slowly slid her finger inside. Pam pushed the vibrator deeper into Charlotte, as Joey went further into Charlotte's ass. She slowly pulled out, continuing to lightly massage her tight anus.

Charlotte felt that wonderful feeling of

what she called "warm fuzzy" all through her belly. Joey then took the beads, inserted the small one in Charlotte's rectum. Twisting it slowly, Charlotte felt the pressure within her. Gently, Joey continued to press the beads in one at a time. Each one was larger, and Joey pushed them ever so slowly until they popped into Charlotte.

With each larger bead, Charlotte groaned in pleasure as they filled her. The more that went in, the greater was the contact with the vibrator Pam was using, allowing Charlotte to feel everything pulsating all the way up to her stomach.

Charlotte pulled her legs closer to her body forcing her ass further into the air. Joey sat in front of Charlotte, spreading her legs by Charlotte's face. Raising her face, Charlotte buried her mouth into Joey's naked pussy pushing her tongue deeper and deeper, as Joey pressed yet another bead into Charlotte's now highly-extended ass. Pam flipped to her back and lay under Charlotte's now full pussy. Pushing the vibrator in, she lifted her head and sucked on Charlotte's extended clit. Charlotte let out a loud groan that was slightly muffled by her mouth being full of Joey's pussy.

The largest bead was now halfway into Charlotte's ass. She relaxed and pushed against Joey's hand until she felt it pop in, filling her completely. The fullness was a fantastic feeling of pleasure, as it all rubbed against the vibrator now deep in her vagina.

Charlotte began to tremble, as Pam worked both on and in her pussy. Grabbing the end of the bead chain, Joey began to slowly pull them out as she spread her own legs further, giving Charlotte more area to put her tongue.

Pushing hard on the exiting beads, Charlotte felt an ecstatic release every time one of them escaped her ass. Lifting her head from Joey's pussy, she began breathing deeply, allowing each exhale to be a deeper moan. As Joey began to pull the beads out faster, Charlotte grasped her own breast, pressing her throbbing pussy onto Pam's hands and face. Finally, unable to hold back, she let out a scream that just kept coming. Popping out the last bead, Joey wrapped her arms around Charlotte, holding her tight as orgasm after orgasm ran through Charlotte's body. Pam pulled out from under and the three women tightly wrapped their arms around each other.

Across the room, the three men applauded loudly. "Now that was a beautiful, fantastic, and never to be forgotten show," Brad hollered. "That went well beyond just sex, it was like art."

"I don't know what it was," Pam said from beneath Charlotte's shoulder. "All I know is I will never ever back down again."

"Can we come play now?" CK asked.

Charlotte rolled over and opened her arms. CK, Brad and Mark joined the women on the king-size bed. Charlotte held CK close, feeling the heat of his now full erection. "It appears you enjoyed our little training exercise." She laughed as she gently held his stiffness.

"You, woman, are driving me crazy," CK moaned quietly as he held Charlotte close to his body. His fingers moved down her back, squeezing her ass.

Charlotte spread her legs and felt him slip his fingers over her moist pussy lips, spreading them lightly. She kissed him deeply, as he moved deeper into her. "Go into me for a minute," she whispered breathlessly, "and then put on the condom."

She spread her legs, as CK rolled between them, lightly kissing her breast. She felt his erection slide down her belly and move between her legs. As the tip of his dick touched between her lips, he slowly moved into her. "Oh yes," she whispered, and then kissed him deeply. He slid his tongue in her mouth as he intensely penetrated her vagina. Pulling away, he pressed deeply into her as he looked into her eyes.

"You feel like paradise," he whispered as he drew back and then pushed deep again. She knew she was losing control and wanted him to fuck her now.

"I need you *now*," she moaned. Looking him in the eyes she whispered, "Just go in my ass. I want to feel you cum in me."

Pulling out, CK pushed her legs further back, and then pressed his dick on her wet ass. He pushed in slowly as he felt her natural resistance, then slid in as she relaxed and took him in deeply. "Oh god, fuck me," Charlotte moaned. "Fuck me now."

CK pushed deep into her ass and pressed his body on her clit. He took her hand, placing it on her clit as he continued to move in and out of her. She began to rub harder as he pressed in and out of her ass.

Pulling her legs back to her head, she pressed on her clit and shoved her fingers deep into her pussy.

She could feel his dick slide in and out of her rectum, as her fingers touched his hardness, while he moved faster and faster. She could tell by the heat of his erection in her ass, he was ready to explode. Charlotte pressed down on her clit, sensing the rush move through her body.

"Oh, yes, yes, yes!" she screamed, shoving her ass toward him. Suddenly she felt him explode within her as she lost control of her own feelings. With a muffled scream, she pushed her ass so he entered the full length of his rock-hard dick into her.

She felt him continue to release within her, then slowly his erection began to soften until he finally pulled out.

Cupping her breast in his hand, he kissed her nipple lightly. Holding him close, Charlotte finally looked over his shoulder and saw Joey sitting on the bed looking at her.

Mark was holding her as she gently stroked his hard cock, but the look on her face was only for Charlotte. Joey smiled and finally said, "That my love, was beautiful."

Charlotte gave CK a hug and quietly

said, "Kind of enjoyed it myself."

Chapter 9

Standing naked before the mirror, drying her hair, Charlotte perused her body with her eyes and decided she was happy with what she saw.

In her undergrad and high school years, she'd been active in sports, especially track, in which she did hurdles. The discipline of sports provided a taught figure, which sometimes bordered on muscular. Her marriage and subsequent divorce played havoc with her athletic body but the last couple years repaired most of the damage.

Now she was a trim size six, with a nice pair of breasts, and a tight ass to boot. Her only complaint was her nose, which she wished was smaller and more petite.

Everyone, including Joey, expressed that she was crazy and her nose was great, but she had her own thoughts that never seemed to change. She leaned into the mirror to get a better look at it and to see how she might restructure it someday.

"Don't tell me you're doing your nose thing again," Joey exclaimed from the bathroom door. "There you stand, buck-ass naked, looking fantastic, and all you can do is worry about a nose that any woman would be happy to call her own!"

Charlotte smiled and turned to Joey, "How about Miss 'My Pussy Lips Are Too Big'? Everyone, especially those of us who have intimate contact with those lips, will all tell you they are fantastic, but you still complain. So let me have my nose, and you can have your pussy lips."

Joey laughed and threw her arms around Charlotte. "I guess we're both a little crazy, but at least we know how to have fun!

You really got a good fucking with CK!"

Charlotte brushed out her hair and thought back on the wonderful time with CK. He was a gentle lover, however he was also a powerful male who knew what to do at the right time. Her rule about 'no condom, no penetration' disappeared with her passion. Nevertheless, she also felt safer with anal penetration, even thought she still had some concern. Whatever the facts, nothing she could do about it now, so on with the show.

"Yep," she finally replied to Joey, "we had a great time together. I hear the music, so I guess the party is now on the second floor."

They'd determined the Rooftop Resort Hotel had a nightclub open on Saturday nights, which catered to those who enjoyed the open lifestyle and sexual freedom of life. She and Joey participated in what they called a "Swingers Club" when the two of them visited Atlantic City. It had a nice dance floor and served some upscale food to all who visited. There was a membership fee, which made it a private club but, as she remembered the fee was minimal.

They'd met a couple of women at the club, ended up on the second floor, in a large bed, having fantastic sex, and providing entertainment for those who watched. Charlotte had been hesitant about having others watch, but as the sex increased, she relaxed with it, actually finding it a turn-on to have others in the room looking at them.

"What goes on at this club?" she asked Joey. "Is it like Atlantic City?"

"I have no idea," Joey replied as she finished her make up, "but I'm sure we'll find out soon. I'm going with the open-back yellow tonight. What are you wearing?"

Joey pulled on a short, yellow dress that was cut down to the top of her ass. The back was laced with gold chains, giving it a very sexy and alluring look. The front plunged down, and gave Joey's expensive new breasts plenty of room to express and show.

"Think I'll go with the black one tonight." Charlotte stepped into a very short black dress that clung to her muscular ass like paint. The material above draped from a lace collar, giving the dress a sleek look, yet providing a lot of flesh exposure as Charlotte moved.

The sides were open so the front and back fell in perfect form, but when she moved they separated, giving maximum, yet brief, exposure of her body. Joey looked at her and then slipped her arms under the material. "Remember," she said softly, "the last dance is mine."

The line was a reminder to both of them
that they had primary allegiance and
responsibility to each other. If either one
of them said it was time to go, then the
other would immediately comply without
question, knowing that the request was a
cover for something being wrong. Their
respect and love for each other had protected
them often, and no matter what was going on,
they knew the last dance of the night was
always with each other. Charlotte kissed Joey
lightly, looking into her beautiful green
eyes. "I got your back, honey, I love you and
always will."

Joey smiled, gave Charlotte's breast a
squeeze and then kissed her again. "I love
you too, baby, so let's go see what trouble
we can get in and out of tonight."

Laughing, the two women stepped out of

their room into the sight and sound of the music and conversation below. Looking up, they could see the stars in the beautiful Florida sky, feeling the warmth of the breeze as it flowed over the roof and into the courtyard. Looking over the party below, they saw the flashing lights, milling people, gyrating dancers, and general high-energy flow. Heading down the stairs from their room, they entered the club, finding it a welcome coolness compared to the night air above. Several cool-air units poured reviving winds down on the dance floor, giving the outdoor club an indoor acuity.

Joey and Charlotte were properly attired, as all the women wore some type of undressed fashion. A few had decided to skip the dress and simply wore high heals and pearls. Typically for this type of affair, the men were dressed in street casual, with either dress shorts with shirt or in some cases slacks.

Charlotte followed Joey to the bar as she worked her way through the people, giving hugs and hellos to many. It was a BYOB bar, so they'd opted to bring a bottle of SKY Vodka and both worked off of it. They found Manny behind the bar along with a beautiful redheaded woman they hadn't met.

"Wow, you two look great," Manny hollered out as they approached.

"You say that to all the women here." Joey laughed as she handed Manny their bottle.

"No, just to those who really deserve it, and you two definitely deserve every compliment I can find. Charlotte, Joey, this is Loretta," he said as he gave the redhead a gentle hug, "She is a great person, great lover, and also a great wife. I know, because she is mine."

They exchanged greetings as Charlotte found herself mesmerized by Loretta. She was about five feet eight inches, a wonderful size four, with milky-white skin, green eyes and the most breathtaking red hair that flowed over her shoulders and down her back. She was topless behind the bar and had the most perfect breasts that appeared to be totally natural. "My god, Loretta, you are beautiful," Charlotte expressed, suddenly being concerned about saying this so loud.

Loretta threw back her head and smiled, "You are soooo much the same, that I am breathless." Saying this she handed Charlotte her drink and blew her a kiss.

"I see you've made friends with Loretta," a voice said behind her. Turning, she saw it was CK and gave him a giant embrace followed by a deep kiss. "Whew," he said as he pulled back, "now that is a warm welcome."

"I just wanted to express my appreciation for our time together a few hours ago. You definitely know how to make a woman happy." Charlotte smiled at CK; however, she knew her strong reaction to CK was a complete surprise to her and one she attributed to her brief encounter with Loretta. The desire that rose up in her as she exchanged a few words with Loretta was almost supernatural, as it literally flushed her skin and took her body temperature up a few degrees. Not understanding her reaction, she decided to let it go and simply have a good time at the party.

CK ordered a drink and then led Charlotte to a table nearby. Charlotte looked around for Joey but lost her in the throng that now packed the bar area. After being seated, she leaned back and began to observe the people around her, most of whom were couples. She saw a lot of the people she and Joey had talked to during their stay at Rooftop, however, there were also a lot of new faces. The DJ was doing a good job of providing music and direction to the assorted guests, allowing several dancers on the floor the freedom of both dance and sex at the same moment.

Looking on the other side of the dance floor she spotted an attractive woman performing oral sex on the male next to her. On the other side of the woman there was a different man who was massaging her breast from behind.

She watched as the woman enthusiastically pursued the stiff penis before her. The people sitting around this sexual encounter seemed to pay it little attention, as they continued with conversation seemingly unconscious of the intense ritual taking place nearby.

Charlotte turned to observe the wall of rooms to her right. Leaning toward CK she asked, "What goes on in the rooms?"

He leaned close to her ear so she could hear his answer. "The one on the left is a play room with a sauna, large leather-covered bed, and a swing designed for sexual pleasure. The next room is a large bed, several small couches and a bathroom with a shower. I think they rent it out as a private room when the hotel isn't having a party here in the club.

Pointing to a large room with a picture window he continued, "The next room is a buffet with snacks, sandwiches, and other food the hotel provides for the guest."

Charlotte put her arm around CK and

hollered above the music, "You're a good tour guide. I guess you have intimate knowledge of the rooms."

CK laughed and stood up. "Just the buffet room. Come on, let's dance for a while."

Charlotte joined him on the dance floor as the music moved into an intense Latin beat bringing more dancers to their feet. She discovered that CK was a good dancer who followed the Latin beat with pure body rhythm.

They were soon in sink with each other, and several dancers stopped to watch them on the floor. Charlotte loved to Samba, and CK easily followed her movement, turning her at the right time, and then moving around her as they followed the heavy beat of the music.

Charlotte felt someone grab her from behind and looking down she recognized Joey's finger rings. Turning, she watched as Joey gyrated to the music, providing a very provocative dance that slowly forced her skirt over her ass.

Joey continued to move around the floor as Mark attempted to keep pace. The dress finally rode all the way up to her waist, so she simply grabbed the hem and pulled it over her head. Handing it to Mark, she freely moved her now naked body across the dance floor, moving to a hot Latin rhythm that truly fit her personality and love of life.

The dancing continued, with Charlotte and CK providing a well-coordinated routine, drawing applause and cheers from the assembled guests around them. The air-conditioned room remained comfortable unless you were dancing with concentration. At that moment, Charlotte felt the perspiration run down her naked back and decided she needed a break.

She nodded to CK that she was finished for now, and then she exited the floor to find a seat along the sidelines. Every place seemed to be taken until CK gently took her hand and led her into the room on the side. It took her a minute to acclimate to the darkness, as CK guided her to a couch along the wall. The AC was delightfully cool in the room, and she was able to recover from the dancing.

"You, my friend, are a great dancer," she said as she leaned back on the couch, allowing the cool air to refresh her moist skin. "I love Salsa, and you took me through every move I knew and added a few new ones."

He had somehow rescued their drinks from the previous table and carried them into the room. "I love dancing, and Latin music is just a part of my soul. Don't know where, but

I know I have Latin blood someplace in my DNA."

Glancing around the darkened room Charlotte noticed there were several other couples in various places around them. Two other couples were sitting in the coolness, while another was on the bed rapidly moving toward a full sexual experience.

Charlotte smiled thinking how casual she'd become with the amount of sexual activity around her. Staying at the Rooftop Hotel, being naked, having sex and feeling relaxed seemed to go hand-in-hand.

Near the door, she spotted a woman who seemed to be going through a gynecological exam with her OBGYN. She was naked, on her back, legs spread in stirrups, with a male providing oral intercourse to her widely-exposed pussy.

"Did you ever try the swing?" CK asked,

as Charlotte continued to stare at the couple.

"No, I thought when you said the room had a swing you meant a real swing, not a stirrup chair," Charlotte replied, continuing to watch. Soon the woman began to groan and then, arching her back, she let out a deep cry as her body gave way to a wave of orgasm.

"Damn," Charlotte exclaimed, "that really worked on her. Never had my OBGYN do that to me."

"Did you ever fantasize about it?" CK asked.

"To be honest, there have been moments when I thought my doctor might be a young, gorgeous male who would violate me as I lay there, but my doctor has always been a nice, but not sexy, older male."

"Hello, Charlotte. My name is Dr. CK, I'll be doing your exam today."

For a second Charlotte didn't understand what CK was saying, but then she caught on and looked at him. Finally, she smiled and said, "Thank you, Dr. CK, I look forward to your examination."

Leading her to the now empty swing, he unsnapped the collar on her dress and pulled it up over her head. Setting the dress on the chair, he grasped her right breast in his hand and massaged it gently. "Everything feels like it's okay, but I must check the nipple to see if it is properly responsive."

Taking her erect nipple, he gently sucked it into his mouth. Charlotte felt the tingle go from her nipple straight to her groin and let out a little short breath as she felt her heat rise. CK repeated the process with her left breast and finally said, "Good news Charlotte, your breasts are beautiful and responsive. Let's now examine

119

your pelvic area to be sure you're totally healthy."

Charlotte sat on the seat and was a little startled when it moved. "That's why they call it a swing, sweetheart," CK said as he held it tight and helped her lay back. "Now let me help you into the proper position."

Removing her shoe, he lifted her left leg, drew her foot up to a stirrup and secured it around her ankle. Charlotte could see it was loose enough if she wanted to get out she could, but decided she was way too turned on to walk away now.

CK lifted her right leg and repeated the securing motion, leaving Charlotte on her back with her legs spread wide, totally exposing her pussy to anyone who walked by her. CK pulled up a chair between her legs and began to stroke her exposed area. "I'll check to see if your vital clitoris response is working." Saying that, he pulled her lips apart and lightly placed his finger on her clit. She felt the fire hit her where he touched and knew her clit was working fine.

Continuing to fondle her gently, he leaned forward in order to place his tongue on her now swollen member. He gently circled her erect clit with his tongue, spreading her lips as he slowly pushed in his finger. The deeper he went, the faster his tongue moved until Charlotte knew the end was near.

Arching her pussy into his mouth, she let out a gasp, feeling her vagina contract as the orgasm flooded over her. He continued to suck on her clit until she finally relaxed. Sliding his finger out he stood and came around to her side.

"Everything seems to be in order, but I am concerned about one thing and need to make one further test." Saying this he slid off his shirt and stepped out of his shorts. He was erect as he slipped open a condom and slowly rolled it out over his hard dick.

Moving the chair from between her legs, he stepped close to her, rubbing his hard cock on her now wet and open pussy. She felt him between her lips, as he slid slowly into her open vagina. Pleasure filled her as she watched him enter deeper and deeper. A few people had gathered around them, and she realized their watching her getting fucked was a tremendous turn-on.

"Now we will run our final exam," CK said, entering her at a more rapid pace. Charlotte held the rope above her as CK moved the swing back and forth, penetrating her now soaking vagina. The impact of the swing on both of their connecting bodies sent waves of ecstasy through her clit and up to her breasts.

CK moved the swing faster and harder, pulling her body deeply onto his cock as he pushed back between her legs. Breathing became difficult as the level of Charlotte's passion increased with each thrust CK drove into her. She dropped her hands to her breasts and squeezed them, feeling his steel-hard erection begin to swell even larger within her.

She experienced the pain of her fingers digging into her breasts as she opened her mouth and gasped out, "Fuck me, oh shit, fuck me now." With a last gasp, she felt an explosion start at the bottom of her feet and move like lightning up her body. Her vagina contracted as she felt CK explode, causing an eruption from within her, literally imprisoning her body in a frozen, paralyzed state, until it released into wave after wave of ecstasy.

She felt him withdraw from her, but was unable to move a muscle in her body. Slowly she opened her eyes, finally letting go of the now painful grip she had on her breast. CK came to her side, kissed her, then placed his open hand over her pussy and pressed down. A spasm of pleasure shot through her until, at last, she felt her body slowly come back to life.

"I thought you might have one more in there," CK whispered in her ear.

"I guess I did, but I'm sure my lungs and stomach may have fallen out of my vagina just now. Holy shit, that was a ride and a half. I've never cum like that, and I'm not sure I'll ever be able to again."

He helped her sit up, then lifted her off the swing, and carried her to a couch. Setting her down gently he said, "I've never enjoyed a climax like I did that one, and I'm not just telling you that to make you happy. Watching you was an experience I've never been through. The more you tensed, the more your muscles took turns swelling and contracting. You are in great shape, my fantastic woman, but the best strength is inside you. When you tensed your vaginal muscles, I thought I would explode, and when I finally did, it was all I could do to keep standing."

He smiled and kissed her lightly on her lips. "Thanks, Charlotte, you're a very special woman."

"And you, sir," she smiled, "are a very special and sexy man, who I enjoy thoroughly. Thanks CK, this is a great weekend because of you."

Chapter 10

After recovering from their swing experience, CK suggested they head back to the bar for a drink. Charlotte decided to join those who had already opted out of clothing and gave her dress to CK, who went to deposit their clothes in a locker. Over half the guests were now either naked or close enough that Charlotte didn't feel out of place. The temperature near the bar was warmer than the "swing room," so the lack of clothing was both sensual and comfortable.

"Charlotte--over here." Charlotte looked toward the far side of the bar and saw Joey waving to her. Working her way through the crowd was interesting as there were abundant naked breasts and buns to squeeze through on the way. One hand did grab her ass for a moment, but Charlotte couldn't locate the culprit in the multitude of bodies. She smiled when she finally reached Joey. "Whew, that's an obstacle course with a few groping hands."

"I know," Joey exclaimed over the noise of the music, "some guy introduced himself and then asked me if I wanted to fuck! Told him yes I did, but not with him. I love the sexual freedom, but there are still limits. Hey, where did you disappear? Looked all over for you."

Charlotte described her romp on the swing and Joey made her promise to take her there later. She then introduced her to an attractive woman sitting next to her. "Charlotte, meet Starr from Hollywood." Joey laughed and gave Starr a hug. " I love saying that!" Joey exclaimed and then explained that Starr was actually named Patricia, who was

127

from Hollywood, Florida, but Joey had decided to call her Starr.

Patricia was an athletic-looking woman who appeared to be in her early forties. Her golden-brown tan gave her a very sexy allure. Between interruptions, Charlotte picked up that Patricia was there with her husband but had somehow misplaced him. She didn't appear overly concerned and was much more intent on being with Joey than finding her husband.

Charlotte turned around to order another drink and locked eyes with beautiful Loretta who was tending bar. *What is it that so captures me with this woman?* Charlotte wondered as she ordered a drink. Watching Loretta move behind the bar, Charlotte actually felt her own body start to respond with sexual desire. She smiled as Loretta handed her a glass. "Loretta, you captivate me," she said as she leaned over the bar. "I don't normally respond like this, but I'm really turned on by you."

Loretta leaned over and gave her a kiss. "Thanks, honey," she said quietly, "coming from you, that's a major statement." Charlotte was about to reply when someone else called out for Loretta, and she moved on down the bar.

"Are you and Loretta an item now?"

Charlotte turned as CK asked the question.

"This is the strangest thing," Charlotte replied. "I'm so intrigued by her; I actually told her she turned me on, and believe me, that's not my normal pattern."

CK leaned in close to Charlotte. "So when you first met Manny what did you think about his sexual orientation?"

Charlotte thought for a minute and then answered, "Honestly, I figured he was gay. No reason, but his mannerism seemed to indicate a more feminine side. He was still a flirt to Joey and me, so I didn't think much about it."

"Well, your first assumption was right," CK said. "Manny is gay. Not bi, not asexual, just full-out gay."

"Wait," Charlotte said, staring at CK, "if he is full gay, then Loretta is…."

Smiling, CK nodded and said, "Yep, Loretta is a shemale."

Charlotte turned and watched Loretta as she worked the bar. She was the most beautiful woman Charlotte had ever seen, and standing there with her naked breasts, she was the most desirable Charlotte could imagine. However, strip Loretta down and suddenly she became a he. Taking a sip of her drink, Charlotte tried to imagine what it would be like to have intimacy with Loretta.

Turning to CK she asked quietly, "Can she get an erection?"

"From what I understand, that is a woman with a totally functional male package," CK replied. "She didn't have a sex change and legally is still a male, but she just loves being a woman. Why, are you interested in having sex with her?"

Charlotte didn't answer immediately. Loretta was beautiful, sexy, and obviously, Charlotte felt a connection. However, was she ready for something like that? The more she thought about it the more intrigued she became. It was like the best of worlds: a beautiful woman and a beautiful dick. Then Charlotte wondered, what would Loretta want from her? Obviously, oral sex would be in order but was that what Loretta wanted as a woman?

Charlotte let out a sigh. "I love the

thought, but I think it may be more complicated than I'm ready to try. Maybe some other time."

Turning back to Joey, she observed Patricia sucking on Joey's breast. Charlotte had witnessed Joey with other women and always appreciated the beauty of the interaction of their bodies. Watching her with a man the other night was also a moment Charlotte enjoyed greatly. Considering this, Charlotte was caught up in the question of why she never felt jealousy when Joey was with someone else. True, they didn't have any permanent commitment to each other, and what either of them did was purely out of their individual desires, nevertheless, Joey was very special to Charlotte, and she loved her deeply.

Yet, when Joey was with someone else, Charlotte always enjoyed Joey's pleasure, basking in the sheer beauty of Joey having sexual fun. She leaned over and gave Joey a kiss, "I love you very much. I'm drunk, thinking way too much, and heading to the pool for a swim. Are you okay?"

Joey brushed the hair from Charlotte's face and smiled. "You are a little wasted aren't you? I love you so much and I'm fine. I think I may have to take 'Starr from Hollywood' to bed soon, so if you come back, we may be there." Looking over Charlotte's shoulder she smiled. "But I have a feeling you and CK may be together when the sun comes up. He may have the last dance tonight, but you and I will be the ones to go home together. Have fun, honey; I'll catch up with you later."

She kissed Charlotte and returned her attention to Patricia. Charlotte smiled as she took CK's hand and led him to the elevator for the Rooftop pool. Joey was truly her best friend ever, and she was also very insightful. Tonight would end with CK, probably in his bed. After laying on a swing with her legs spread apart, everything else seemed tame and reasonable.

Chapter 11

The morning sun greeted Charlotte as she rolled on her side toward the window. A great desire for darkness attempted to pull her from the bed and force her to close the curtain. However, the painful thought of moving into an upright position finally triumphed over the need for darkness, so she simply turned away from the window. That move brought her face to face with another individual.

Suddenly realizing she was not in her own room, Charlotte sat up, focused on the sleeping body next to her, and determined it was CK. Slowly she returned to a reclined position, attempting to piece together the previous night's activities.

When Charlotte determined she had too much to drink and needed a swim to sober up,

she and CK journeyed to the pool. The roof
area was quieter than the club with only a
few couples in the water and others scattered
among the lounges. The two of them spent
quite some time in the water talking and
enjoying the beautiful Florida night. She
remembered they also enjoyed some beautiful
intimate activity in the water but had
stopped short of actually having intercourse.
Or had they? She didn't remember all the
details but felt safe in trusting CK.

Trusting — that was a word she hadn't
contemplated in some time. She trusted Joey;
they knew and loved each other. But trusting
a man was something she hadn't even
considered since her divorce. Sitting up on
her elbow, she looked at CK sleeping next to
her. He was a beautiful man with a very
gentle disposition, a combination she admired
yet found difficult to find in others she'd

met. She knew one thing for sure, this man was a great lover possessing the ability to touch places in her passion she'd never experienced. Reaching over, she slowly pulled back the sheet until he lay naked before her. He moved slightly, throwing his arm over his head and rolling onto his back.

Looking down his tanned body, Charlotte was fascinated to see his erect cock rising from his stomach. Smiling, she wondered what erotic dream he was having, and if she was part of it. Quietly reaching over, she lightly touched his hardness, letting her hand drift down the shaft and rest between his legs. Running her fingers around his testicles, she felt her own passion grow.

Squeezing her thighs together, she once again slipped her fingers around his hard shaft, moving them up to the tip, and then holding it tight. CK didn't move as Charlotte massaged him, so she moved closer until she could hold his cock and lightly run it over her face and down her neck. Caressing it loosely, she looked at the blood vessels throbbing up the shaft toward his circumcised head. Leaning forward, she placed it on her lips and lightly touched her tongue to the tip. Parting her lips, she slowly slid it deep into her mouth. CK stirred for a moment, then continued to rest quietly.

Charlotte quietly ran her tongue around the throbbing dick, sensing the softness of the flesh as it stretched tight. Deep in her mouth, she felt the tip touch the back of her throat just before she withdrew it and held it before her eyes. Running her fingers up the now wet and gleaming shaft, she felt her own passion rise deep in her groin.

Reaching down, she ran her free hand between her pussy lips that were now wide and wet. Spreading her legs, Charlotte slipped inside as she simultaneously took CK's hard cock back in her mouth. Leaning over him, she moved her fingers deep in her very receptive pussy as she continued to suck on his dick. Sucking hard, she moved faster until she felt the edge of climax in her body. Releasing CK, she grasped her pussy tightly, exploding in hot satisfaction. She held her hand in place as the ripples went through her body and then released her grip.

Looking up, she saw CK looking at her with a sleepy grin. "You seem to be having fun," he said quietly.

Rolling over toward him, Charlotte once again took his erection in her hand and smiled back, saying, "I have only just begun."

Moving to her knees, she slipped between CK's legs and lowered her head to meet his cock. Spreading his legs, CK let out a quiet groan as Charlotte took him into her mouth and started to stroke him, running her tongue around all his sensitive areas. Moving her hand faster, she sucked on him and held his dick tightly in her mouth, her tongue moving around him. Sliding her head up and down, she felt his dick become even harder in her mouth.

Moving faster, she sensed his body becoming rigid as he thrust hard into her tight, moving lips. Tasting the first early discharge, she knew he would explode soon. Tightening her lips, she ran her tongue faster around his head, while squeezing hard with her hand. Feeling the pressure in the palm of her hand, she released it and took CK deep in her mouth, as he erupted in orgasm. She tasted the bitter saltiness of his cum, as his body shook below her. Then he relaxed, and she slowly pulled him out of her mouth until he had completed every bit of his release.

"Son of a bitch," he moaned, "I don't think I ever felt an orgasm from my toes to my head."

Laughing, she placed her head on his chest. "I loved it too."

Listening to the sound of his heartbeat, she joined him in a quiet morning nap, as the sun continued to fill the room with the new day.

Chapter 12

Charlotte leaned back in the seat, watching the green tropic of Florida disappear beneath the wing of the jet. Closing her eyes, she slowly reviewed the events of the weekend and once again marveled at the life she now lived. Every time she moved into something new and different, it became a starting point for her next adventure. She smiled as she contemplated how the next adventure could possibly top this last weekend.

Between Thursday and Sunday she'd spent about ninety percent of the time naked. She'd participated in more sexual activity in three days than she would normally have in three weeks. How in the world would she ever top that?

She thought about CK and the great morning they spent together after the first wake-up oral escapade. He was a fascinating man who possessed a great deal of knowledge about the fine art of making a woman feel satisfied.

They made plans to meet again in a couple months, but this time he wanted her to come to Tampa and stay at another clothing-optional resort near him. Unlike most, "we have to do this again" promises couples make after a good time together, Charlotte decided she would actually follow up on this one and meet CK again in Tampa. He was the type of man who may help her truly believe in the positive aspects of relationships, but the only way to find out would be to spend more time together.

"What are you smiling about?" Joey asked as she leaned close to Charlotte. "Thinking about all your wild activities this weekend?"

Charlotte looked at her deeply-tanned

friend and smiled. "You need to live in Florida. You are even more beautiful now that you're rested and tan."

Joey took Charlotte's hand and laughed. "I may be more tan, but I'm not sure I'm rested. My little party with Patricia lasted until sunrise."

Charlotte hadn't caught up with Joey until noon, and then they had to pack and leave for the airport to catch their flight. Between saying goodbye to everyone, catching a taxi to the airport and getting on the flight, they hadn't had a chance to review the activities of the night before.

Charlotte leaned closer to Joey. "Do tell."

"Patricia was a nymph!" Joey chuckled, "I thought she would eat me alive! I took her back to our room, and she attacked my pussy from every angle possible. I think she gave me oral sex for almost two hours. On about my fifteenth orgasm I finally had to push her off so I could catch my breath. I mean, I loved it, but it was a bit much."

Charlotte laughed, "I doubt if you complained too much. What happened then?"

"We took a break and went up to the pool. You'd already left, but we ran into Patricia's husband who was entertaining some woman in the pool. We joined them and somehow ended up in the swing room you told me about."

"Did you try the swing?" Charlotte asked conspiratorially.

"On my back, legs in the air, and Patricia back on my pussy." Joey laughed.

"Then I became a smorgasbord for the collected multitude of players gathered around the room. Patricia's husband fucked me, as well as the woman he was with, who I still don't know if she had a name. Then my buddy Mark showed up and finally rescued me. We ducked out of the room and headed back to our room where we spent some wonderful time until I finally fell asleep. It had to be close to six; the sun was already up."

Charlotte laughed. "You wild woman; I leave you alone for a minute and look what you get yourself into without me."

Joey squeezed Charlotte's hand. "I missed you, but you seemed to be into CK pretty deep."

"We had a fantastic time. He is really a wonderful lover and a truly nice guy."

"OH OH!" Joey exclaimed. "Is Charlotte starting a relationship?"

"I don't think so, but I'm open to see him again. He wants us to come to Tampa and stay at another place he knows there."

"Us?" Joey asked, looking at Charlotte.

"We come as a package deal or we don't come at all," Charlotte said seriously. "You are part of me, and CK knows that."

"I know," Joey said as she leaned back, "but there will come a time when someone else will probably be in our lives, and we have to face that as a fact. I really love you, and I know you feel the same, but our lives have to move on sometime. Guess whoever we do end up with will just have to understand that what we have is part of the deal."

"Probably true," Charlotte said, looking at Joey and smiling, "but for now, you are still the only person in my life."

Joey kissed Charlotte lightly. "That is the truth for me too. Guess what I got for you?" Joey reached into her purse and pulled out a paper bag, which she handed to Charlotte. Opening it, Charlotte pulled out two bottles containing some type of liquid.

Looking at Joey she gasped, "Is this what I think it is?"

"I ran into Lee and persuaded him to give me some of the Island Magic Oil."

"Oh my god, can't this plane fly any faster?" Charlotte exclaimed.

Joey laughed and raised her glass of Coke. "Here's to a great weekend, a lot of fun, and the promise of a wonderful night together."

Charlotte raised her glass, "To my wonderful friend and our crazy life together. Let the adventure continue!"

The End

If you enjoyed this story, join "**J**" on her web site www.J-Erotica.com as she takes you on an adventure into the world of love, romance and sexual pleasure. The journey of sensuality continues in her new book;

Carpe Diem

A moment of pleasure

The following is an excerpt for your enjoyment.

Chapter 1

The computer screen taunted Sandy as she felt the pangs of desire move through her body settling mainly between her legs. It was warm in her apartment yet she knew the perspiration between her breasts wasn't from the furnace; at least not the one in the basement of her apartment building.

The hollow light of the Internet video flooded the space as she watched the sexual equipment on the well-hung male became larger before her eyes. The cause of this transformation was mainly from the concerted effort of a big-breasted blonde female kneeling and sucking on his manhood. Sandy felt her pulse quicken as his gleaming, wet, steel rod appeared on her screen. Rubbing the perspiration from her forehead, she watched as her Stud Man took the blonde and threw her on the bed. Sandy's breathing became shorter as Stud Man aggressively pulled the blonde's legs apart and stood over her naked body stroking his huge dick.

"That thing is enormous," Sandy muttered, quickly looking around to be sure nobody heard her. It was a stupid move; her only sex partner tonight was the flashing computer screen that mocked her empty life with putrid fantasy. Feeling a sense of futility, she reached to turn off the program just as Stud Man began to push his enormous rod into the blonde's glistening pussy. Hesitating, Sandy waited to see if he could actually get it inside the small opening presented by the blonde. The camera moved closer to the action, while Sandy's hands moved from her laptop to her lap. Spreading her legs, she began to touch the flimsy material confining her now screaming pussy.

The camera closed in on his steel-hard dick as it began to penetrate the female's folds of skin. Pulling out, his dick now glistening with the wetness of the blonde's deepest recesses, Stud Man spread her lips further apart and then pushed in deeper and deeper.

Sandy felt the cloth under her fingers become moist as she rubbed a little harder.

Sliding them aside, she spread her own wet
lips and slowly began to run her fingers up
and down the slick, hot space demanding her
attention. The blonde pulled her legs further
back as stud man penetrated her with the full
extension of his massive erection, forcing
Sandy to push into her own beckoning vagina.
Unable to reach deep, she stood, pulled off
her underpants, sat down in the chair and
spread her leg on each side of the computer
screen. The flashing strobes of light
flickered on her naked garden of pleasure as
her fingers danced over the sensitive places
that sent electricity through her body. Using
her free hand, she pulled her T-shirt over
her head, threw it off and began to message
her breast, pushing deeper into her throbbing
vagina.

Stud Man now turned the blonde over,
positioning her ass in the air. Spreading her

cheeks, he rubbed his huge dick on her quivering vagina and then shoved into her violently. Increasing his tempo, the blonde's tits began to sway with the impact of his fucking, as Sandy pushed inside into her own playground. Feeling her fingers getting wetter, she dove deeper trying to maintain the same rhythm as Stud Man. Releasing her breast, she moved her free hand to her clit and exposed it to her touch, discovering it was very hard and very needy.

Stud Man continued to slam away at the blonde who was definitely in the throws of orgasmic delight. Sandy pulled her legs back, frantically rubbing her pulsating clit. She felt pressure inside her build until she sensed splattering on her legs and ass. Her garden of pleasure was about to become a river of orgasm that would soak her body and floor; she chose to ignore the outpouring of her passion.

Stud Man was sweating and banging harder as Sandy felt the growing pangs of orgasm build in her groin. "Hurry up," she groaned, trying to hang on to her climax until Stud Man came. At last he pulled out, turned the blond over, and rapidly stroked his erection over her bulging tits. Sandy grabbed her pussy, jammed her fingers deep inside, and frantically rubbed her clit until at last she and Stud man both ejaculated into the world around them. While his load fell on the naked breasts of the blonde, Sandy's fell into a large puddle below her chair as it ran down her ass like a river. Leaning back she slowly brought her feet to the floor trying to avoid the wetness below. It didn't happen often, but when she was overly horny, she became a waterfall that would soak everything around her.

Walking to the kitchen, Sandy glanced at her naked reflection in the mirror. Things had improved over the last two years. She no longer cringed at the woman in the mirror who'd somehow grown into a rapidly aging, overweight, divorce-ravaged victim. She'd vowed to recover her lost self and two years of therapy, dieting, gym workouts, and freedom from the piece of shit known as her ex-husband had contributed to the woman she now viewed before her. At forty-two she'd regained her waistline coupled with trim hips, nicely rounded ass, and well-proportioned, natural breasts. She wished her tummy was muscular but settled with the fact that it was soft yet flat, an okay exception at her age. Her dark hair was a return to her pre-blonde days, and she liked how it framed her green eyes. Thinking about the blonde in the video, she was happy she'd returned to her natural dark color.

Turning from the mirror, she journeyed into the kitchen, picked up the role of paper towels and then headed back to clean up her vaginal-river remains. Throwing the towel pieces on the floor, Sandy once again looked at her computer screen observing the other twenty-four videos offered, all of which provided a stimulus for those who needed to masturbate through their sexually-empty lives. Closing the laptop, she picked up her wet underwear and hastily discarded shirt. With a deep sigh she headed to her bed. As usual with her Internet sex parties, she felt even emptier at the end than she had at the beginning. For the millionth time, Sandy vowed she had to do something about her empty sex life. Turning out the light, she drifted into a discontented sleep.

To order copies of J's books go to

www.Amazon.com or use the link to J's web

site http://WWW.J-Erotica.com

To explore the adventure of Rooftop the **Rooftop Resort Hotel web site is** www.Rooftopresort.com

The largest lifestyle website, with over 2 million members around the world is SDC. This is their link http://www.SDC.COM

www.ingramcontent.com/pod-product-compliance
Lightning Source LLC
Chambersburg PA
CBHW071344170626
46811CB00003B/986